This Little Tiger book belongs to:

_____

_____

_____

_____

For Ben and Tom, with love
~ J. R.

*For Ethan, who surprised
everyone by being so early*
~ T. W.

LITTLE TIGER PRESS
An imprint of Magi Publications
1 The Coda Centre, 189 Munster Road, London SW6 6AW, UK
www.littletigerpress.com

First published in Great Britain 2005 by Little Tiger Press, London
This edition published 2008

Printed in China

2 4 6 8 10 9 7 5 3

Rosie's Special Surprise

Julia Rawlinson   *illustrated by* Tim Warnes

LITTLE TIGER PRESS

Rosie liked to know everything about everything, but Daddy Rabbit was planning a special surprise. Rosie kept trying to guess what it could be, but Daddy Rabbit only smiled and said, "Wait and see."

But Rosie couldn't wait. While the other rabbits were napping one afternoon, she hopped out of the burrow.

Rosie hopped across the stream, up the hill, and through the meadow.

Brushing buttercups,
over the clover, under
the sun she hopped.
Around the big tree,
past a small tree, and
over a log she hopped.

And behind the
log she found . . .

a bunch of acorns hidden
in a fallen hollow tree.

"That's not your surprise," chattered
a scampering squirrel.

"Do you know what my surprise is?" asked
Rosie, bouncing up and down.

"Yes. It's shaped a little bit like an acorn,"
said the squirrel. Then he scampered off with
some twigs, and Rosie hopped on.

She asked the butterflies and
the bees if they'd seen her surprise.
She asked the sheep and the cows
if they had seen it.

She asked the mice and
the moles if they had seen it.
And as she was asking the
moles she saw . . .

a secret entrance to the moles' tunnel.

"That's not your surprise," snuffled the burrowing moles.

"Do you know what my surprise is?" asked Rosie, hopping around.

"Yes, we do. It's not a tunnel, but you can go into it," said the moles. Then they burrowed off to work on their tunnels.

Rosie searched under stones
and snail shells and bits of twig.
She searched through the dappled
sunshine of the forest.

She searched among the
scraggly tangles of the brush.
And in the brush she found . . .

a nest full of blue eggs.
"That's not your surprise,"
chirped Mommy Bird.

"Do you know what my surprise is?"
asked Rosie, sniffing the breeze.
"Yes. It's blue, a little bit like our eggs,"
said Daddy Bird as he fluttered to the nest.

Rosie hopped along, up a steep hill. She found a stone shaped like an acorn, but that wasn't her surprise. She found a fern-covered den that she could go into, but that wasn't the surprise, either.

She found a flower as blue as
a bird's egg, but that wasn't it.
Where could her surprise be?
Rosie stood up on her tiptoes.
She looked out over the
woods and . . .

tumbled down,
down, down the hill.
Rosie rolled head-over-heels.
Bumpity-bump, up in the air and
down on her tail fell Rosie. Slipping and
sliding, skidding and skittering, with four paws
flying, she tumbled.

Rosie finally landed in a heap, with a bump and a thud and a last little thump.

Then she sat up, twitched her ears, and gave a sad little sniff. "I'm never going to find this thing," she said, brushing dirt from her fur. "I'm tired of looking and hopping," she said, rubbing her bumped bunny nose.

"Too tired for your surprise?"
asked Daddy Rabbit, hopping up.
"Come with me and see . . ."

"your huge blue balloon of a surprise!
Jump in and ride with me."

"Ooh! Thank you, thank you!" said
Rosie, jumping in.

"Now I can see
the whole wide
world! I can see . . .

"EVERYTHING!"

fantastic reads from Little Tiger Press

THE LONG JOURNEY HOME
David Bedford and Penny Ives

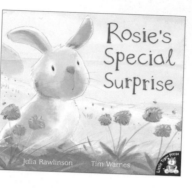

Rosie's Special Surprise
Julia Rawlinson   Tim Warnes

SLEEP TIGHT, GINGER KITTEN
Adèle Geras
Catherine Walters

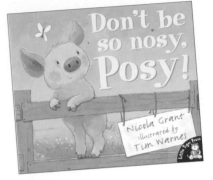

Don't be so nosy, Posy!
Nicola Grant
illustrated by
Tim Warnes

Sleepy Sam
Michael Catchpool
illustrated by
Eleanor Taylor

Don't Be Afraid, Little One
CAROLINE PITCHER
PICTURES BY
JANE CHAPMAN

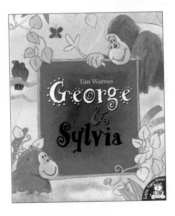

Tim Warnes
George & Sylvia

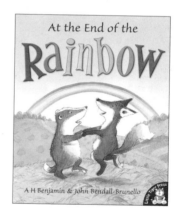

At the End of the
Rainbow
A H Benjamin & John Bendall-Brunello

for information regarding any of the above titles
or for our catalogue, please contact us:
Little Tiger Press, 1 The Coda Centre,
189 Munster Road, London SW6 6AW, UK
Tel: +44 (0)20 7385 6333 Fax: +44 (0)20 7385 7333
E-mail: info@littletiger.co.uk
www.littletigerpress.com

Clever Little Freddy
Christine Leeson   Joanne Moss

One, Two, Three, Oops!
Michael Coleman
Gwyneth Williamson